Reach for the Stars

A Little Torah's Journey

(Based on a true story)

By Sylvia Rouss
Illustrated by Rosalie Ofer

in cooperation with Professor Joachim H. Joseph

PITSPOPANY

NEW YORK ◆ JERUSALEM

Other books by Sylvia Rouss:

The Littlest Pair
2002 Storytelling World Award Winner
2002 National Jewish Book Award Winner

Tali's Jerusalem Scrapbook
2003 Sydney Taylor Honor Award Winner

The Littlest Frog

The Littlest Candlesticks

Reach for the Stars: A Little Torah's Journey
Published by PITSPOPANY PRESS
Text Copyright: ©2004 Sylvia Rouss
Illustrations Copyright ©2004 Rosie Ofer
Design: Rosie Ofer

Hard Cover ISBN: 1-930143-82-6
Soft Cover ISBN: 1-930143-83-4

Library of Congress Cataloging-in-Publication Data

Rouss, Sylvia A.
Reach for the stars : a little Torah's journey / by Sylvia Rouss ;
in cooperation with Joachim H. Joseph.
p. cm. Summary: The story of the miniature Torah that was taken by Israeli astronaut, Ilan Ramon,
aboard the ill-fated Columbia Space Shuttle.

ISBN 1-930143-82-6 — ISBN 1-930143-83-4 (pbk. : alk. paper)
1. Torah scrolls—Juvenile literature. 2. Ramon, Ilan, 1954-2003—Juvenile literature. 3. Joseph, Joachim-Juvenile literature.
4. Dasberg, Simon—Juvenile literature. 5. Bergen-Belsen (Concentration camp)—Juvenile literature. [1. Torah scrolls. 2.
Ramon, Ilan, 1954-2003. 3. Joseph, Joachim. 4. Dasberg, Simon. 5. Bergen-Belsen (Concentration camp) 6. Columbia
(Spacecraft) 7. Space shuttles—Accidents.] I. Joseph, Joachim. II. Title.

BM657.T6R68 2004
296.4'615—dc22

2003024206

Pitspopany Press titles may be purchased for fund raising programs by schools and organizations by contacting:

Marketing Director, Pitspopany Press
40 East 78th Street, Suite 16D
New York, New York 10021
Tel: (800)232-2931
Fax: (212)472-6253
Email: Pitspop@netvision.net.il
Website: www.pitspopany.com

Printed in Israel

Dedication by Sylvia Rouss

This story is dedicated to the memories of the seven astronauts who lost their lives aboard the American space shuttle Columbia, on February 1, 2003 – Rick Husband, William McCool, Michael Anderson, Kalpana Chawla, David Brown, Laurel Clark, and Ilan Ramon. They were remarkable human beings who risked their lives for the betterment of mankind.

It is also dedicated to the memory of Simon Dasberg, Chief Rabbi of Amsterdam, Holland, who lost his life in the Bergen-Belsen concentration camp. Rabbi Dasberg used a little Torah, which he had smuggled into the camp, to train a young boy for his Bar Mitzvah. Later, he entrusted the Torah to the young boy. He had no way of knowing that the little Torah would one day have such an impact on a people, a nation, and the world.

Thank you to Professor Joachim H. Joseph of Tel Aviv University. He was the young boy, Yoya, who rescued the little Torah and made this story possible.

No. 55946/Ifa   **IDENTITY CARD**

Name of holder JOACHIM   יואכים

JOSEPH   יוסף

Signature of holder   יואכים

Place of residence

KIRYAT-HAIM   ק"ח-ג"ק

Place of business

Occupation PUPIL   תלמיד

Race Jew   גזע

Height 5 feet 10 inches

Colour of eyes brown   חום

Colour of hair

Build tall   גבוה

Special peculiarities

Signature of issuing officer

Appointment

Place   Date 8.

Possession of this card is no way implies evidence of legal residence in Palestine.

DISTRICT

Introduction by Joachim Joseph

My name is Joachim Joseph, but you can call me Yoya. I am the one who gave the Israeli astronaut, Ilan Ramon, the little Torah scroll he took with him on the space shuttle Columbia, on January 16, 2003. It was given to me by Rabbi Dasberg in the Bergen-Belsen Concentration Camp during the Holocaust.

Ilan and I were good friends, and when I gave him the Torah scroll I felt as though the little Torah would finally reach the Heavens it had come from.

Ilan was born in 1954 and lived in Be'er Sheva, Israel, where he graduated first in his high school class. His father came to Israel from Germany before WWII, and his mother arrived in Israel after the Holocaust, straight from the terrible Auschwitz Concentration Camp.

Ilan was married to Rona, a lovely and vivacious Sabra, a native Israeli, and they had four children, three boys and a girl. He was a natural pilot and became an ace in the Israeli Air Force where he flew all types of fighter planes. He took part in many dangerous and exciting missions, including the bombing of the Iraqi nuclear facility. During his service with the Air Force, he also studied at Tel Aviv University and graduated as an electronics and computer engineer.

Ilan was a small man, but when he walked into a room, everyone noticed him. He had a twinkle in his eye and a way of presenting himself to people that made you want to be his friend as soon as you met him. He was not just a father to his kids but their good friend, too. They always came to him with any problem, task, or question.

In 1998, Ilan was chosen to become the first Israeli astronaut, a dream that he worked hard to make come true. He passed the training program in Houston with flying colors. He trained for five years and finally was given a berth on the space shuttle Columbia on Mission STS- 107.

Ilan rapidly became the focus of the STS- 107 crew. He invited them to his home for dinner on Friday evenings, led them on difficult nature hikes, and became their personal, good friend. He kept contact with the Jewish communities in the USA, and volunteered to travel and talk to communities across the country.

Many people came to see the launch of the Columbia, including myself. It was an extremely impressive occasion. We were three miles away when the space shuttle took off, and yet the shock waves of the launch shook every part of our bodies. The launch was successful, but nobody knew that the left wing had been fatally hit by a piece of debris.

As soon as they were safely in space, all the astronauts took off their space suits, changed into polo shirts and shorts, and started a tough around-the-clock work program divided into two 12-hour shifts. For sixteen days, Ilan was busy 12 hours a day, working on the Mediterranean Israeli Dust Experiment, doing experiments on flaming bubbles floating in space, growing crystals, and many medical experiments.

Ilan enjoyed living in space. He also liked the tremendous views he had of the earth. He sent e-mails to his friends and family on earth and even conducted press conferences from space.

While not an Orthodox Jew, Ilan considered himself to be the representative of all the Jewish people. So, while on the space shuttle, he ate only kosher food, kept the Shabbat, and even made Kiddush. He took a Mezuzah, donated by Holocaust survivors in the USA, with him into space. He also took a picture of the earth as seen from the moon, drawn by a young boy who died in the concentration camps.

And he took a little Torah scroll, whose story you'll now discover.

Ilan Ramon showed the world the tiny Torah scroll that was not much bigger than the palm of his hand. Its red velvet cover was worn, and its scroll had yellowed with age. But as Ilan gently held it, the Torah shone aboard the space shuttle Columbia. It had traveled to space with Ilan and six other astronauts. "This is a small Torah scroll that a young boy received from a Rabbi almost 60 years ago in Bergen-Belsen. The Rabbi used it to train the boy for his Bar Mitzvah and then gave it to him for safekeeping. That boy is Professor Joachim Joseph, a survivor of the Holocaust living in Israel," Ilan told all those listening.

The professor watched the scene from the earth below. How thrilled Yoya – that's what everyone affectionately calls him – was! It seemed like only yesterday that the little Torah scroll was in another time and place.

It had lit up the home of Rabbi Simon Dasberg who lived in Holland with his young family. The Rabbi often shared its stories with his children.

"Tell us how God made the whole wide world?" the Rabbi's little son asked one Shabbat evening.

"In the beginning there was only darkness," the Rabbi slowly began. "Then God made the light. He called the light day and the darkness night."

"Next, God made the sky, and then the land and the oceans," his older son proudly added.

"Yes," agreed his father. "That happened on the second and third days. On the fourth day, God created the sun, the moon, and all the stars and saw that it was good." The four children who were gathered around him looked out the nearby window. Their eyes gazed with wonder at the twinkling stars in the night sky.

"How did God do it, Papa?" asked his younger daughter, tugging at her father's sleeve.

"God is capable of many wondrous deeds." The Rabbi smiled. "How, is not important, but why?"

"Why then, Papa?" inquired his wide-eyed little boy.

Patiently Rabbi Dasberg responded, "Perhaps so that you will reach for the stars and try to find the answer for yourself."

"I think God wants to remind us that He is always near," said his older son thoughtfully.

"Yes," nodded the Rabbi, "that too." Then he continued. "On the fifth day, God made the birds and fish and finally, on the sixth day, God made all other living creatures, even people."

Suddenly, the children heard their mother's voice exclaim, "After completing all that work, God rested on the seventh day and made it holy.

"That's why we celebrate Shabbat each week! And now, it is bedtime for some very tired children."

"We want to hear more," protested the oldest child, a girl with bright rosy cheeks.

"The Torah is eternal. Come, your m o t h e r and I will tuck you in. Tomorrow, I will tell you more."

The Rabbi's wife smiled as she handed each child a cup of warm milk. "Now you shall have wonderful dreams."

The Dasberg home was full of joy and laughter. The tiny Torah was a part of each Shabbat and every holiday celebration. The children loved discussing its stories with their father.

Abruptly, the joy vanished and the laughter ceased. The sound of thunderous rumbling tanks, roaring motorcycles, and hundreds of marching feet made the earth tremble as the Nazis invaded the town.

It was as if a sudden storm was sweeping through the city and destroying everything in its path. Soon, all Jewish children were forbidden to attend the local schools with non-Jewish children. Jews could no longer ride on buses and streetcars or shop in stores owned by non-Jews. When the Rabbi's children asked to play in the neighborhood playground, their father told them that this too was forbidden.

"May we at least take a walk in the park?" his little son pleaded.

The Rabbi sadly shook his head.

One night, the Rabbi's wife sewed yellow stars on the family's clothing.

"What are you doing?" asked her small daughter, curiously.

"The Nazis have decided that all Jews must wear these," sighed the Rabbi's wife.

"A star!" exclaimed her little boy. "Is it to remind us that God is always near?"

"Yes, my child," nodded the Rabbi's wife, tears clouding her eyes. There was no point in frightening the children she thought, as she continued, "Never forget that even in the darkest times, God is near. We must not give up hope that one day the light will return."

The days continued to grow darker. Many Jewish shops were destroyed, Torah scrolls were damaged, and often Jews were beaten or taken away from their families.

Then the day came when the family found out that all Jews would be transported to concentration camps. The Rabbi gathered his family together. He looked at the tear-stained faces of his children who had to leave behind their picture books and games, their dolls and blocks. Almost everything they owned would be lost, but the Rabbi took the little Torah from the shelf and placed it into his traveling case.

"I know leaving our home is difficult. Yet we still have each other. No matter what happens, remember the most important teaching of the Torah: always treat others as you would want to be treated. Don't let these harsh times destroy your love for others. Hold onto your dreams and reach for the stars."

When the family arrived at the Bergen-Belsen concentration camp, they were sent to a section called the *Sternlager* or Star Camp. Here they were separated from each other. The Rabbi went to the men's barrack, while his wife and four children went to the women's barrack. As the Rabbi embraced his family, he told them, "Try to be brave and remember to take care of each other."

"Don't worry, Papa, everything will be fine," said his little son softly. "We are in the Star Camp. God will be near.

The Rabbi nodded as he turned his face away from his wife and children. He gazed with sorrow at the two huge barbed wire fences surrounding the camp. He could hear the fierce barking of the guard dogs that patrolled the area between the fences. It was a terrible place created by hateful men, but he knew that at night the stars would shine to remind his family of the beautiful world God had created.

Life in Bergen-Belsen was very difficult. Everyone had to work, beginning early in the morning until late at night. They were given very little to eat. There was no warm milk for pleasant dreams, only the food of nightmares. A small crust of bread and watery soup was often the only meal for an entire day. Those who were too weak to work were punished by the camp guards.

The barracks were drafty and unheated. Wooden bunks were stacked three on top of each other and lined the barrack walls. Because the barracks were overcrowded, at least two people had to sleep together on each cold, hard bunk. Sometimes they didn't even have a blanket to cover themselves. Some people lost hope, others became sick, and many died.

Rabbi Dasberg shared a crowded barrack with men and boys. There he met Joachim Joseph – Yoya – a young boy who had been separated from his family when they arrived at Bergen-Belsen. Yoya liked to listen to the men talk about Eretz Israel.

"If I leave this place, that's where I will go," stated a tall man with stooped shoulders.

Rabbi Dasberg nodded in agreement. He described the beauty of the ancient land where he had once studied.

"I remember the sweet Jaffa oranges that were shipped to my home," Yoya said quietly. "Maybe some day I can go there and pick my own."

"B'ezrat Hashem, God willing," added one of the men.

Each day, the Rabbi led the men in prayers. When the Rabbi discovered that Yoya was near Bar Mitzvah age, he took the tiny Torah from his traveling case where he kept it hidden.

"Would you like to study for your Bar Mitzvah from this little Torah?" Rabbi Dasberg asked him.

Yoya's eyes widened with surprise. He remembered the large Torah scrolls from his synagogue, but this was the smallest Torah he had ever seen. He nodded his head eagerly.

"We will have to study secretly," the Rabbi cautioned. "It won't be easy."

For several weeks, Yoya learned with the Rabbi. Even when his feet became frostbitten from the icy winter cold, Yoya looked forward to his lessons. After a long, hard day of work, while everyone in the barrack fell asleep, the tired boy and the exhausted Rabbi would remove the tiny Torah from its hiding place and study together.

Many nights before Yoya drifted off to sleep, he would think of the Bar Mitzvah services he had attended at the big synagogue near his home. He remembered the excitement of the young boys when they read from the Torah.

Afterwards there was a big celebration with family and friends. Frosted cakes and cookies were served, and the Bar Mitzvah boy received gifts. Yoya knew his family would not be at his Bar Mitzvah. There would be no presents or rich desserts, but still he could hardly wait.

When the Bar Mitzvah day arrived, Yoya woke up early. He could hear people snoring in their bunks while a storm howled outside. As he climbed out of bed in his bandaged feet, he winced with pain. He shivered from the cold, but his eyes were bright with anticipation. Rabbi Dasberg was already waiting for him near a small table set with four candles, two on either side of the little Torah.

Yoya smiled when he saw the group of men who had gotten up early for this special occasion. Blankets covered the windows so that no one on the outside could see the candlelight. He heard a few men announce to the others, "We'll stand by the barrack doors to keep watch." If the guards found out about the ceremony, everyone would be punished.

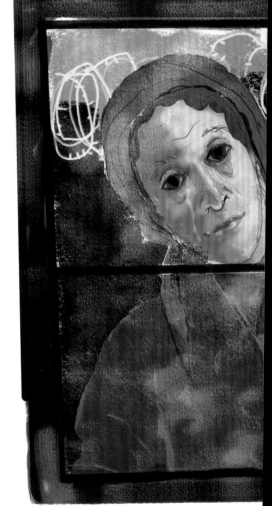

The men started chanting prayers. Suddenly there was a quiet tapping at the barrack door. Everyone froze with fear. One of the men slowly opened the door. An icy blast of air made Yoya's feet throb, but his heart was warmed by the sight of his mother. She had come to share in her son's happiness even though it was forbidden for her to be there. The men in the barrack were afraid to let her enter, so she stood in the bitter cold and listened from the outside.

The service continued as the Rabbi unrolled the scroll and Yoya began reading the Hebrew. For a moment, the men, even with their hollowed faces and ragged clothing, stood strong and proud as they watched the young boy who had worked so hard to become a Bar Mitzvah. When he finished, the Rabbi blessed him and everyone said, "Mazel Tov!"

Yoya went outside to his mother. She was very thin, but her face was flushed with joy.

"I'm so happy for you!" she said, giving him a kiss. She smiled as she continued, "I made you these mittens with a piece of cloth I smuggled out of the workshop. And here, I want you to take my portion of bread."

Tears glistened in Yoya's eyes as he embraced his mother. "Thank you. Please be careful. Don't get caught by the guards." As his mother turned to go, Yoya rejoined the men.

"Come let us celebrate," said Rabbi Dasberg. He gave everyone a sliver of bread meagerly coated with a vegetable spread made from the evening soup.

One of the men smiled at Yoya. "I have a gift for you," he said, holding out a tiny deck of playing cards. Another man gave him a small piece of chocolate.

Yoya's lips trembled as he whispered, "Thank you." He felt overwhelmed by their generosity in this place where personal possessions and food were so precious.

Suddenly, the camp whistle blew. It was the signal for everyone to go to work.

Later that night, Rabbi Dasberg spoke to Yoya as he gently placed the tiny Torah into his hands. "I want you to take this little Torah and keep it safe. I don't think I will survive this place, but you might. Promise me that, if you leave, you will tell the world what happened here."

When the Rabbi blessed him, the boy bit his lip to keep from crying. He thought about the wonderful man who had treated him like one of his own children. Here, in this terrible place, the Rabbi had helped him achieve a dream. He had become a Bar Mitzvah. By placing the Torah into Yoya's hands for safekeeping, Rabbi Dasberg believed that the boy would overcome any hardships to keep his promise. He would reach for the stars.

Yoya wrapped the little Torah in rags and hid it in the bottom of his knapsack. There he kept it safe until the end of the war, when he and his family were reunited. Together they traveled to Israel and, for a time, Yoya lived on a Kibbutz where he once again enjoyed sweet Jaffa oranges. Later, he fought in several wars to defend the Jewish State. He tried to forget about Bergen-Belsen, but the little Torah always reminded him of the promise he had made to Rabbi Dasberg. Eventually he married and had children of his own. Rabbi Dasberg would have been proud to learn that the young boy he befriended at Bergen-Belsen became a Professor of Planetary Physics at Tel Aviv University. He had indeed reached for the stars.

Yoya always kept the little Torah near. Sometimes he would look at it but he never read from it. One day when his grandchildren were visiting, Yoya decided they were old enough to understand. He showed them the tiny scroll and began to tell them his story. The children listened quietly.

After finishing the story, Yoya looked at them and asked, "Where do you think we should keep this little Torah so that you can see it whenever you visit?"

"Let's build a little Aron Kodesh, like the large cabinets where synagogues keep their Torah scrolls!" his granddaughter suggested.

"We can build it out of wood and paint it!" exclaimed his grandson.

"That's a wonderful idea! How did I get such smart grandchildren?" Yoya said. Together they constructed a lovely wooden case. After they painted it, they carefully put the little Torah inside, and placed the Aron Kodesh on the bookshelf for everyone to see.

One day, Ilan Ramon, a young man who had been selected to be the first Israeli astronaut, came to Yoya's home. They began to discuss the experiments Ilan would be researching for Yoya in space. When Ilan noticed the little case, he asked, "What is that?"

"It's a small Aron Kodesh that holds the Torah scroll that I received from a Rabbi in the Bergen-Belsen concentration camp. He used it to train me for my Bar Mitzvah," explained Yoya.

"Will you tell me the story?" asked Ilan.

Yoya began to share his experience while Ilan listened silently. When Yoya finished, Ilan told him, "My grandmother and mother were also in a concentration camp." A deep bond of friendship developed between the two men. They talked about their service in the Israeli army.

"Had there been a Jewish State, the Jewish people would not have suffered the way our families did," Ilan concluded. He recalled how he had trained to become a fighter pilot and how proud he was to defend his country.

A few weeks later, Ilan called Yoya. "I have been thinking about your little Torah scroll ever since I saw it in your home. I was hoping that you might allow me to take it into space.

"Perhaps it will remind all Jews of our historical and religious traditions and will bring our people closer together. Most importantly, I think this little Torah will show everyone the ability of the Jewish people to survive and go from the darkest days to days of hope in the future."

Yoya quickly agreed. "I promised Rabbi Dasberg that someday I would tell the world the story of this Torah. Thank you, Ilan, for helping me keep that promise."

Ilan was excited about the space mission. It was like a dream come true. He moved to the United States and trained at the Space Center in Houston, where he quickly became friends with the six other astronauts. Even though they came from different backgrounds and religions, they treated each other with kindness and respect.

When Yoya came to visit, Ilan introduced him to his new friends. Yoya found the astronauts to be a dedicated and caring team that enjoyed training together.

On January 16, 2003, the space shuttle was finally launched into space. In addition to the small Torah scroll, Ilan also took with him a copy of a drawing, done by a fourteen-year-old boy who had been in the same concentration camp as Ilan's mother.

Although Ilan was not religious, he followed the teachings of the Torah during the flight. He kept kosher and observed Shabbat. He was an inspiration to Jews everywhere.

When he communicated from space, he told those listening, "From up here, Israel appears small and very beautiful. The quiet that envelopes space makes the beauty even more powerful, and I only hope that the quiet can one day spread to my country."

For sixteen days, the space shuttle Columbia maneuvered through space as the seven crew members on board conducted experiments that would help people all over the world.

Sometimes they would marvel at the spectacular view outside.

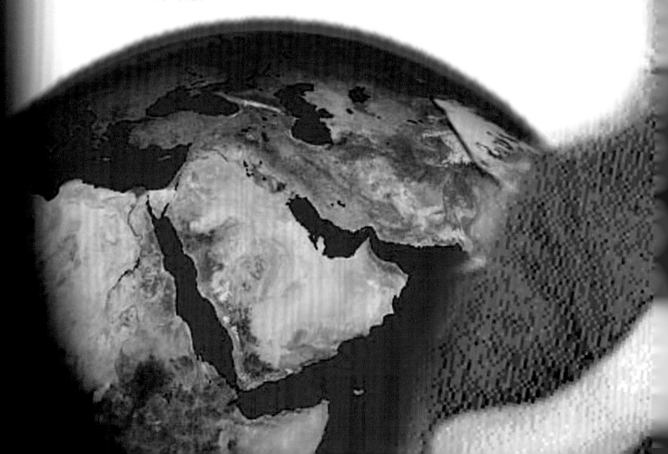

"It's glorious. Even the stars have a special bright-ness!" exclaimed one of the astronauts.

"Drifting through space is like floating on the clouds of a beautiful dream," sighed another.

"Yes," said Ilan, "It's so quiet and peaceful up here."

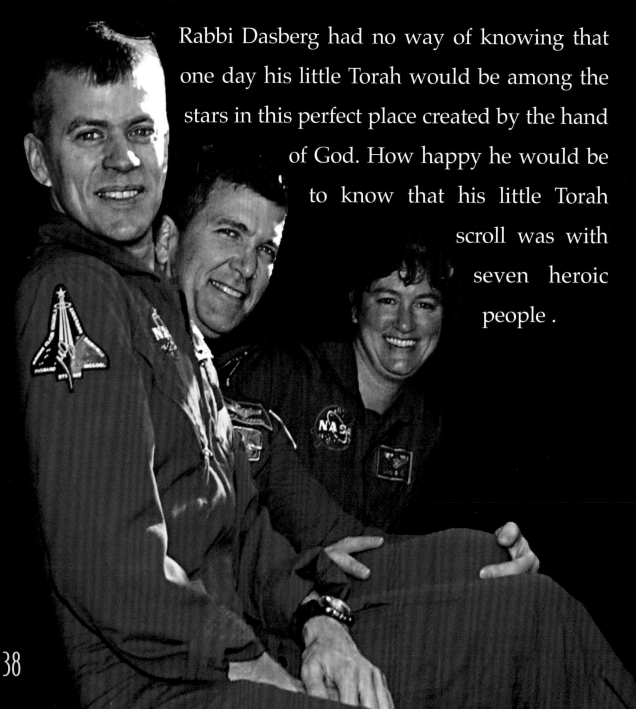

They all looked at the universe with the same wonder that had been on the faces of Rabbi Dasberg's children when they gazed up at the stars. Their joy and laughter was also a pleasant reminder of a time long ago.

Rabbi Dasberg had no way of knowing that one day his little Torah would be among the stars in this perfect place created by the hand of God. How happy he would be to know that his little Torah scroll was with seven heroic people .

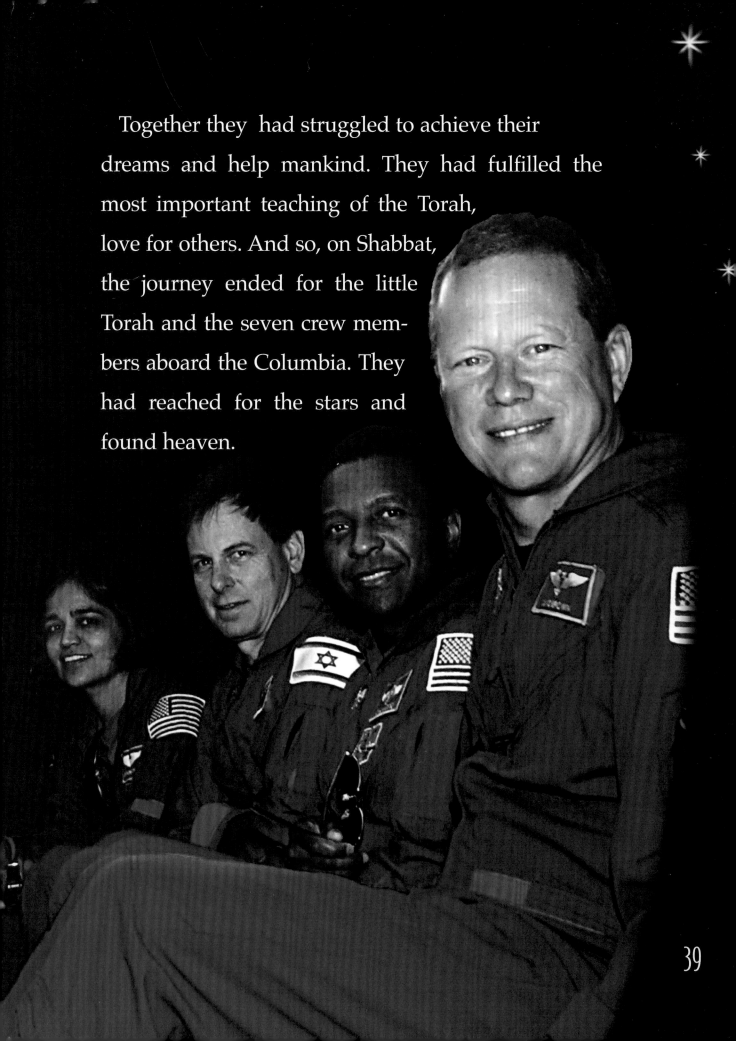

Together they had struggled to achieve their dreams and help mankind. They had fulfilled the most important teaching of the Torah, love for others. And so, on Shabbat, the journey ended for the little Torah and the seven crew members aboard the Columbia. They had reached for the stars and found heaven.

Epilogue

On February 1, 2003, the space shuttle Columbia tragically blasted apart as it re-entered the earth's atmosphere. The seven astronauts on board, including the first Israeli astronaut, lost their lives. Professor Joachim Joseph was watching the descent on a screen at a NASA command center. "I turned away from the screen, feeling that seven pieces were being torn from my heart."

The little Torah that belonged to Rabbi Simon Dasberg was not recovered, but its importance was not diminished. It brought light to Rabbi Dasberg and his family, to Yoya, to the Jewish people and the world.

Hundreds of people from all over the world sent Yoya letters and e-mails of condolences. Many newspapers and television stations published the story.

Three of Rabbi Simon Dasberg's children survived the Holocaust and live in Israel. The Rabbi, his wife, and youngest son all perished.